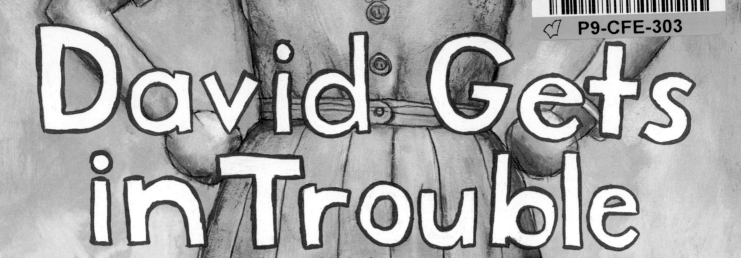

David Gets in Trouble

By David Shannon

SCHOLASTIC INC.

New York Toronto London Auckland Sydney
Mexico City New Delhi Hong Kong Buenos Aires

AUTHOR'S NOTE

A few years ago, my mother sent me a book I made when I was a little boy. It was illustrated with drawings of David doing all sorts of things he wasn't supposed to do, and the text consisted entirely of the words "no" and "David"—they were the only words I knew how to spell! I thought it would be fun to make a new version celebrating all the time-honored ways moms say "no." Like the original, it was called *No, David!*

In the sequel, *David Goes to School.*, David found out that his teacher had her own ways of saying "no."

Well, now it's David's turn to speak, and it turns out that "no" is a big part of his vocabulary, too. Of course, when his mom says "no," it's because she worries about his safety, and she wants him to grow up to be a good person. Deep down, she's really saying, "I love you." But when David says "no," it usually means "I don't want to get in trouble!"

To my little troublemaker, Emma; and to Heidi, her mom, who has to say "no."

This book was originally published in hardcover by the Blue Sky Press in 2002.

ISBN 0-439-05154-1

34 33 32   11/0

Printed in the U.S.A.   40

First Scholastic paperback printing, September 2003

When David gets in trouble,
he always says . . .

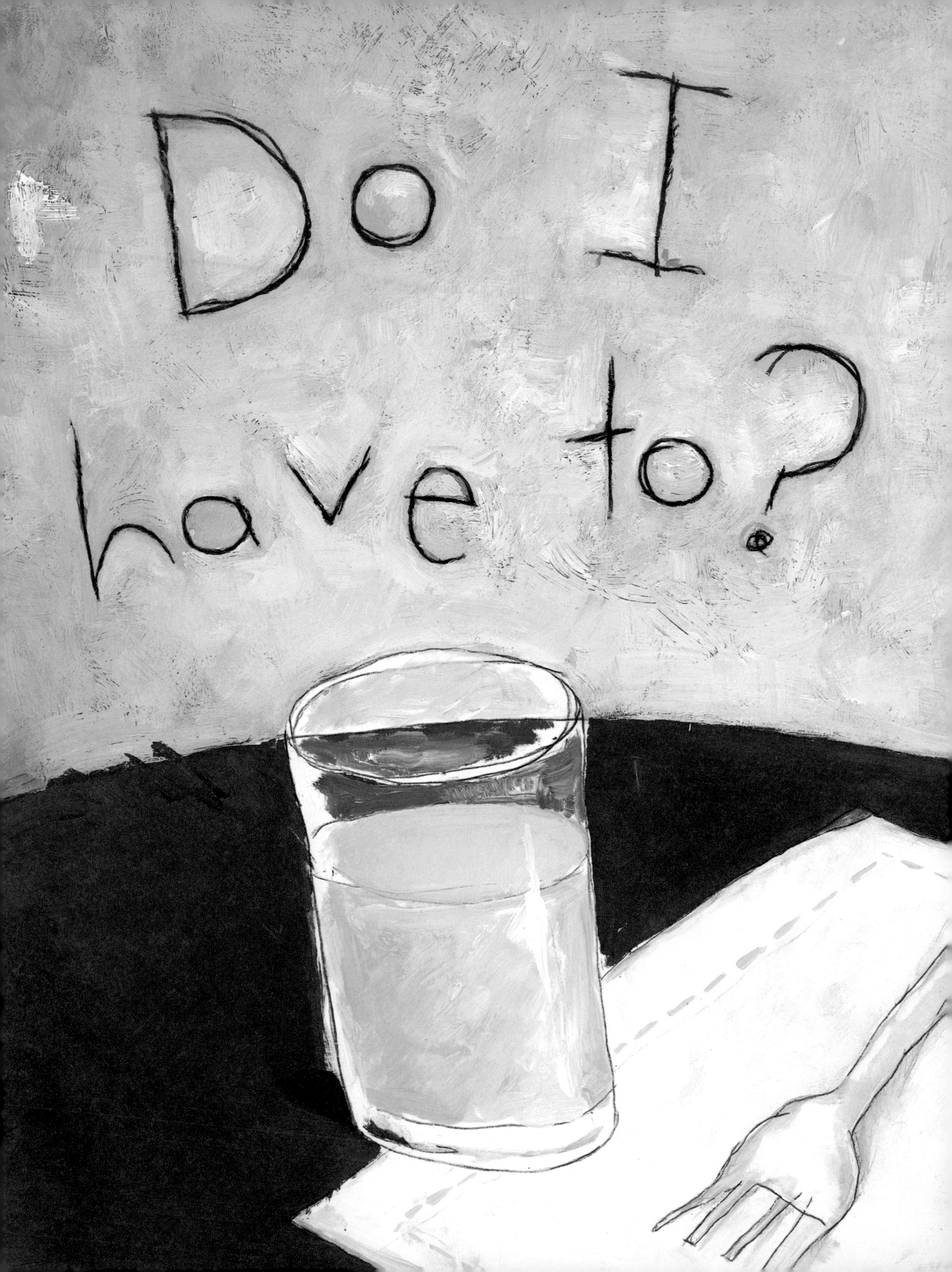
Do I
have to?

I couldn't help

DICKENS ELEME

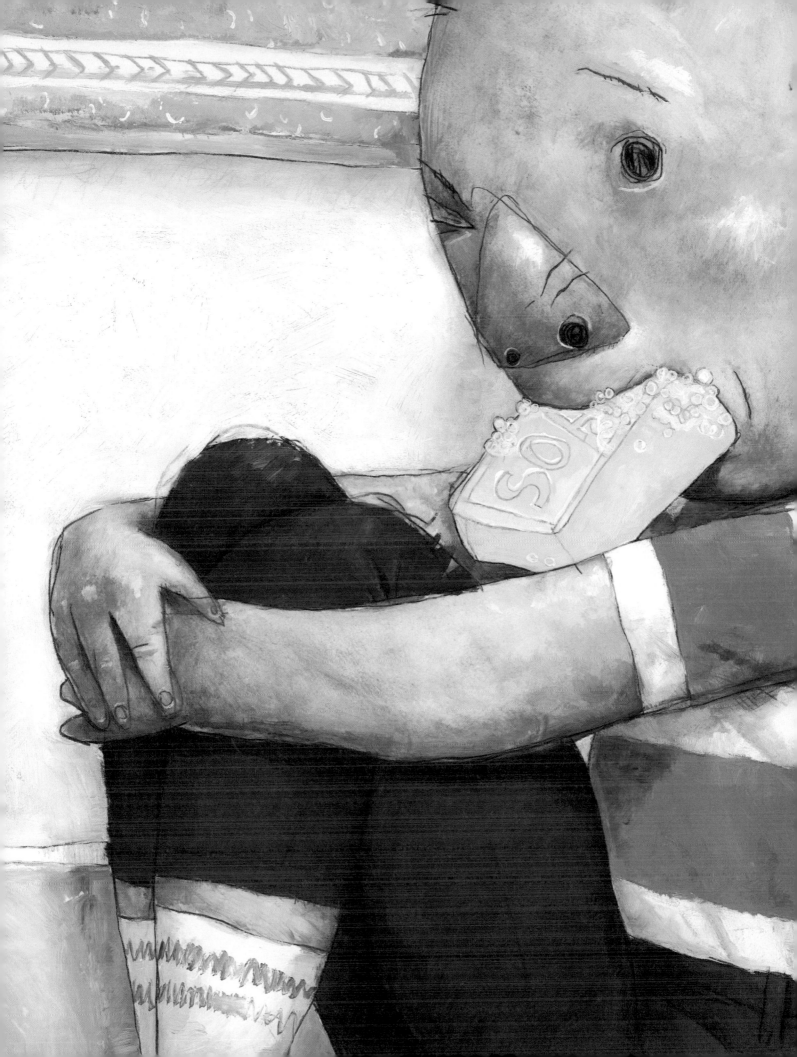

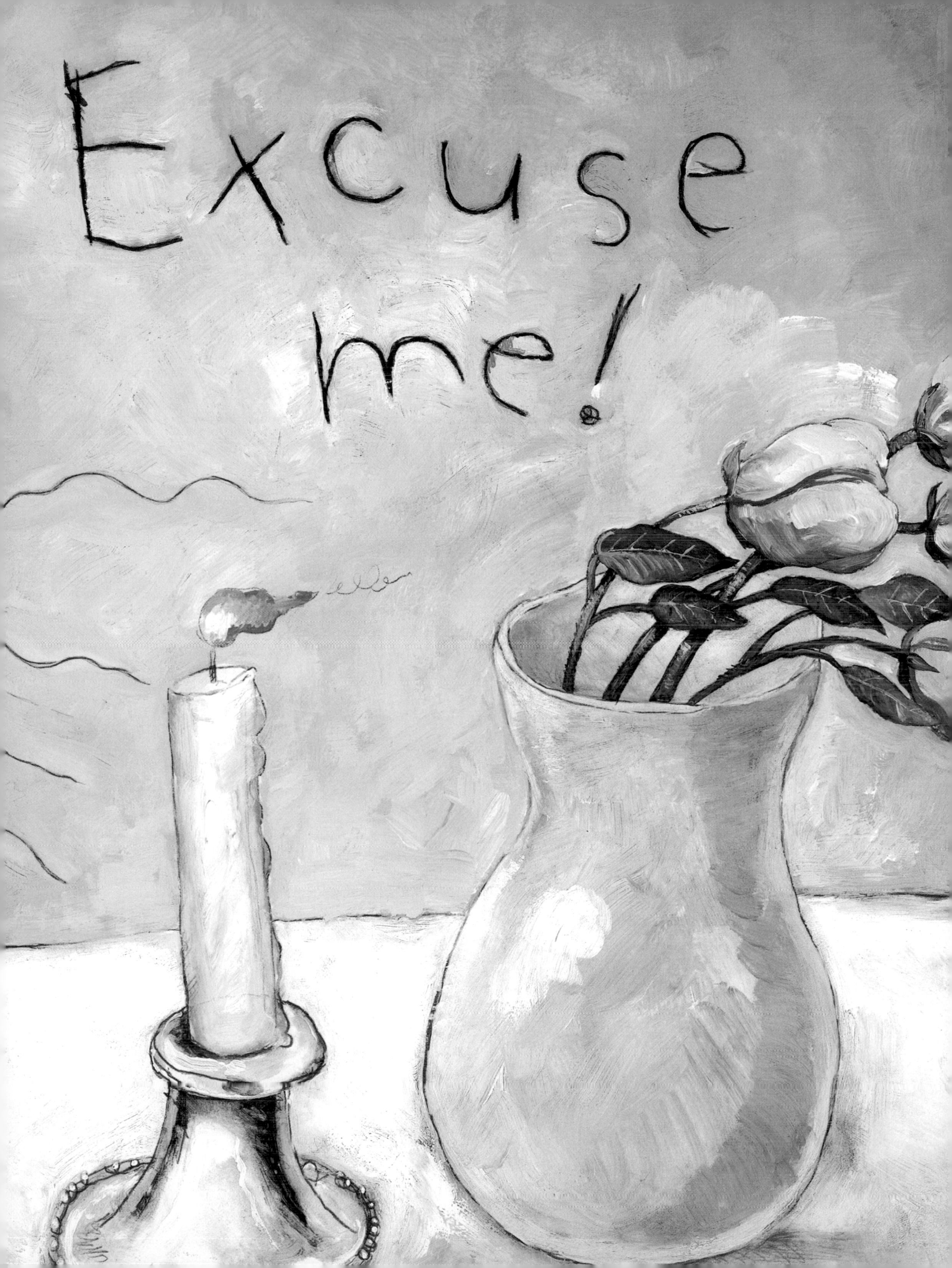
Excuse me!

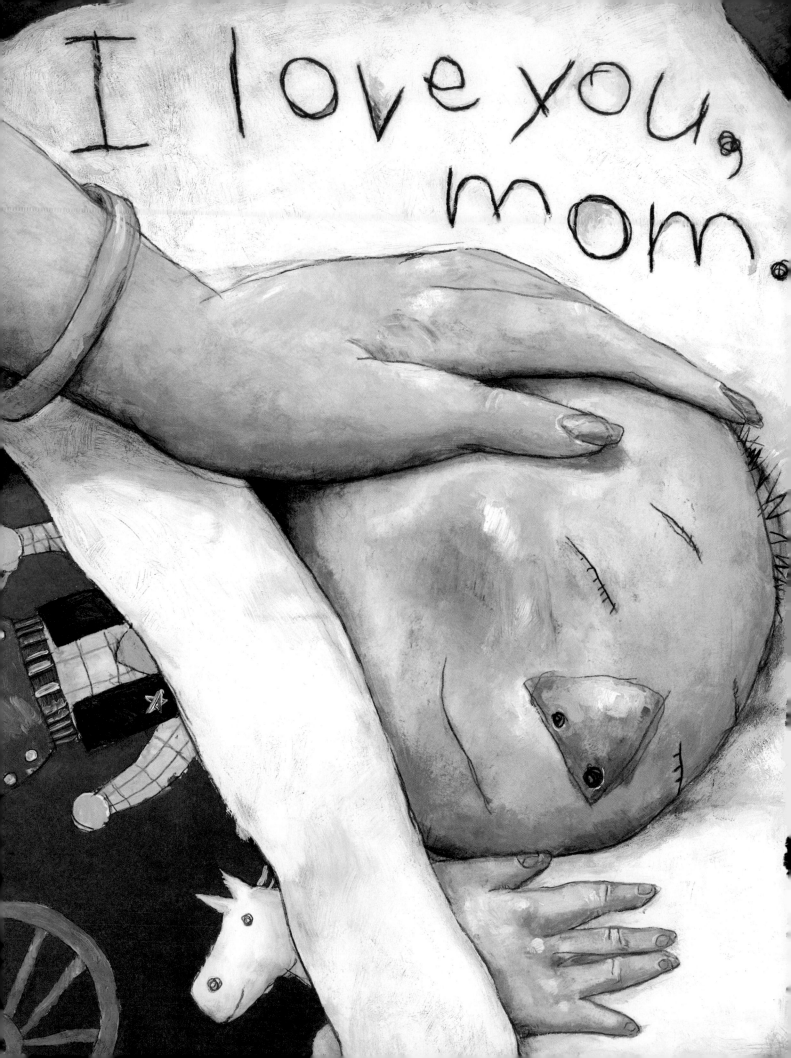